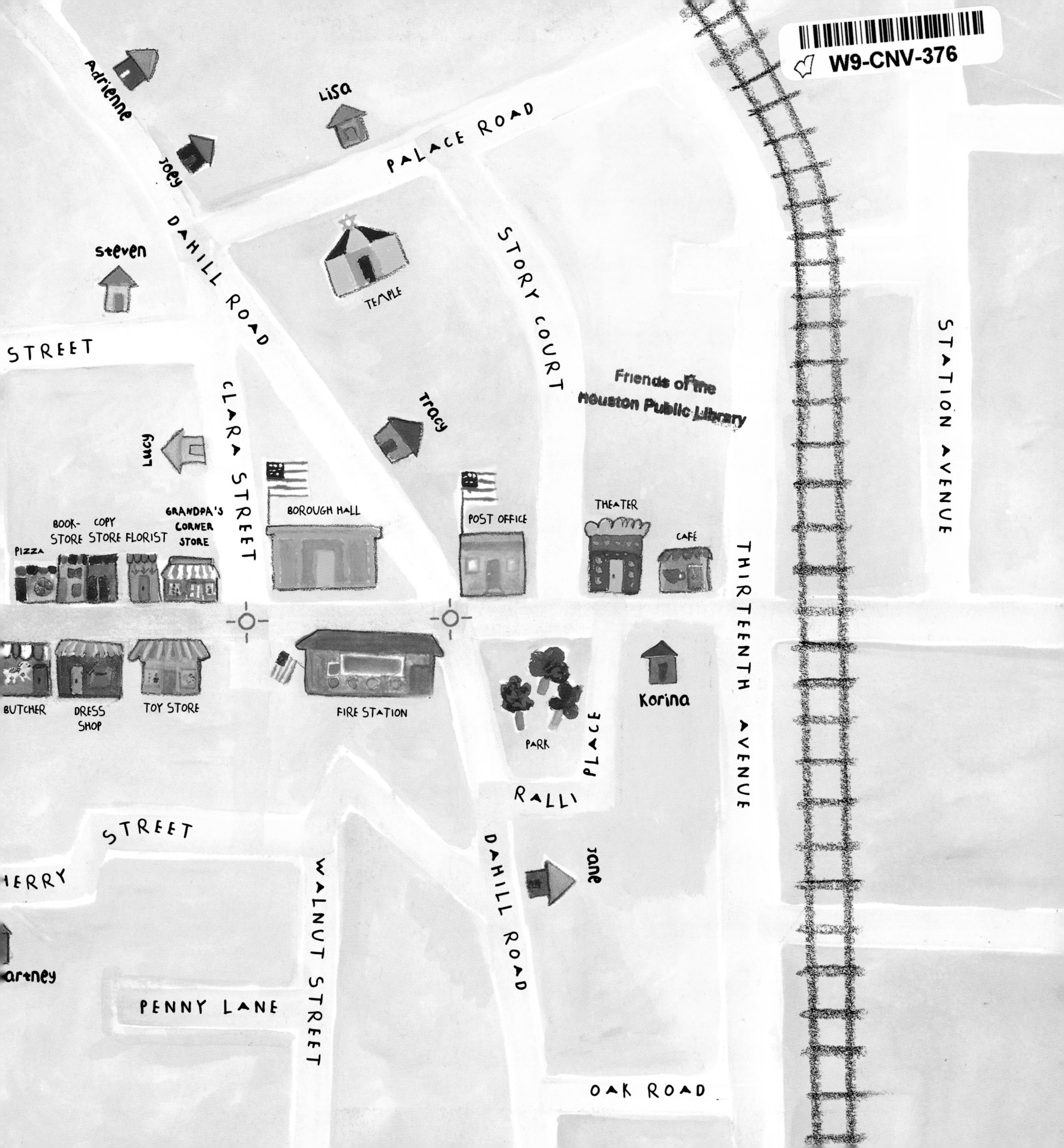
Adrienne
Lisa
Joey
PALACE ROAD
DAHILL ROAD
Steven
TEMPLE
STORY COURT
STREET
CLARA STREET
Tracy
Lucy
STATION AVENUE
BOROUGH HALL
POST OFFICE
THEATER
CAFÉ
PIZZA
BOOK-STORE
COPY STORE
FLORIST
GRANDPA'S CORNER STORE
BUTCHER
DRESS SHOP
TOY STORE
FIRE STATION
PARK
Korina
THIRTEENTH AVENUE
PLACE
RALLI
STREET
IERRY
WALNUT STREET
DAHILL ROAD
Jane
artney
PENNY LANE
OAK ROAD

To Lizzi across the street and Adrianne across the ocean

DyAnne DiSalvo-Ryan

Grandpa's Corner Store

HarperCollinsPublishers

JOE'S COPY STORE
April Florist

MR. BUTLER SOLD HIS HARDWARE STORE when a bigger one opened nearby. Then the building was torn down to make way for a new supermarket.

"Good luck," I say to Mr. Butler as he bumps his suitcase into his car.

"We'll miss you," my grandpa tells him. "*And* we'll miss your hardware store."

I hold on to Grandpa's hand, and we wave until Mr. Butler's car turns the corner.

Old stores are out. New stores are in. But my grandpa's store stays the same. A busy corner grocery with black and white tiles all worn straight down the middle aisle. Milk, juice, butter, eggs—the store has everything you need close by.

Grandpa lives in a room in the back. There's a bed for sleeping, a kitchen for cooking, and a cat named Shirley for company.

Saturday mornings I'm at the grocery to give Grandpa a hand. I stack the cans and sweep the aisles. Kids toss their bikes and skateboards outside and pile inside for candy. Firefighters from across the street line up at the deli counter. Mrs. Kalfo takes their orders and bags them up to go.

AT YUM

"I know, I know," Mrs. Kalfo says. "Cheese and pickle sandwiches. Hers on rye. His on wheat. Extra mayo on yours, right, chief?"

Chief Conley smiles at Grandpa. "She always gets it right."

The store is busy on Saturdays, so my mother comes in to help. Neighbors stop by to pick up what they need—a quart of milk, a box of cereal. Mr. Tutti comes in for yesterday's paper. He likes to take his time when he reads, so Grandpa saves it for him.

"So what do you think? With the new supermarket opening up, are you going to sell your store?" Mr. Tutti says flat out to my grandpa.

"Sell the grocery?" I look at Grandpa. "I don't think so," I tell Mr. Tutti. "My grandpa would never do that."

On Monday morning my teacher, Miss McCartney, tapes our neighborhood map on the board. We paste the library closest to the school, Korina's house farthest from Ira's.

"The new supermarket will have everything," Steven says without even raising his hand.

"My grandpa's store has everything already," I say a little bit louder than Miss McCartney would like.

But whatever I say that Grandpa's store has, Steven says the supermarket will have it too. Cheaper and bigger and better.

After school I stop for a minute to watch the construction work. My ears begin to tingle from the noise. Then all of a sudden I get this feeling that maybe Steven is right. The supermarket *is* going to be big. It was already much bigger than me.

"Lucy's here," Grandpa yells, waiting to give me my three o'clock hug. Mrs. Kalfo takes charge of the register. The table in the kitchen is set for homework, and Grandpa keeps me company. My mother says it's a nice arrangement to have while she's at work. I think so too.

"I'm making your corner grocery store to put on the neighborhood map at school," I say. Grandpa watches me color it in. "Steven is making the supermarket. He says your store is all washed up and you'll be moving to Florida, just like Mr. Butler."

Grandpa sighs and picks up a crayon. "Maybe Florida is nice," he says. "It's not so cold in the winter."

I laugh and give Grandpa a kiss. "Florida's too far away. You can't run your store from there."

When the telephone rings, it's Mr. Lee calling in an order.

"He's under the weather," my grandpa says.

I help pack the delivery bag. Bread, soup, coffee, noodles. Grandpa puts his coat on to go. Some deliveries are special, so he likes to do them himself.

I've finished coloring Grandpa's store when my mother comes to get me. I toss my crayons under the counter just before I leave. That's when I see a red FOR SALE sign hidden beneath some bags.

12.56

I can't even talk on the way home, but when we get inside, the words spill out.

"Is Grandpa selling his store?" I ask.

My mother sits us both in a chair. "Grandpa doesn't *want* to sell. He's afraid the new supermarket will put him out of business."

"Will Grandpa live with us if he sells?"

My mother looks around. "I'd like that more than anything," she says. "But we don't have the room."

I am just about to say he can have my room when I hear a knock at the door. Mrs. Kalfo stands in the hallway.

"Everybody's talking," Mrs. Kalfo says. She flutters her hands like a bird in a nest. "Everybody's worried the store will close."

"We're worried too," my mother says. "Come in. Sit down."

Mrs. Kalfo straightens her hat. "I guess, if it does, I'll try to get a job at the new supermarket. Things won't be the same for me anymore."

I throw my arms around my mother. "We have to do something," I say.

The next day, on the way to Grandpa's store, I try not to notice that the supermarket's going up fast. Construction workers call out to one another, waving steel beams into place. The sky is gray and thick with clouds. It almost feels like snow.

"Cold out there?" Mrs. Kalfo asks me, wrapping up a sandwich. Mrs. Duffy from down the block is huddled up talking to Grandpa.

"Pay when you can," I hear Grandpa whisper. Cheese, milk, diapers, bread.

Mrs. Duffy pats Grandpa's hand. "What would I do without you?" she says.

I bring my homework into the back and wait at the kitchen table.

As soon as Grandpa takes his seat, I ask him about that FOR SALE sign.

Grandpa looks down at the black and white tiles that need to be replaced. He looks up at a crack in the ceiling that needs to be repaired. "The new supermarket will have everything from soup to nuts," he tells me.

"But it won't have *you.*" I hug my grandpa, trying not to cry. I give him the grocery store I colored in for school. "If you're really going to sell your store, then you can keep this," I say. "The map won't need it now."

The Saturday the roof goes up on the supermarket, the FOR SALE sign goes up in Grandpa's window. In school on Monday, I won't even look at Steven. He keeps waving around a flyer he ripped from a pole on the avenue—

SUPERMARKET OPENS NEXT WEEK.

"I hope your grandpa likes Florida," he says, teasing. I grab the flyer out of his hand and throw it into the wastebasket.

We take turns pasting up more buildings. Somebody puts a tag with the words *mud pile* where the supermarket is being built, but Miss McCartney takes it down. I think that somebody is me.

"A community is a group of people who live and work together," Miss McCartney says, pointing to our map.

I think about what our community would be like without my grandpa's store.

And then I look at Steven and smile. Miss McCartney has given me an idea.

"Be there Saturday morning," I tell all the kids on my way home after school.

"Nine o'clock sharp," the firefighters say.

“I’ll help spread the word,” says Mr. Tutti.

“Not a problem.” Mr. Lee sneezes.

Mrs. Kalfo pats my arm. “You can count on me,” she says.

It snows every single day that week. Clouds hang frozen in the winter sky like sheets dried stiff on a clothesline. But that doesn't stop the supermarket from opening up on Saturday. Colored flags snap in the wind. SPECIAL! SPECIAL! SALE TODAY! My mother and I yank on boots, pull down hats, and head for Grandpa's store.

"I hope this works," I tell my mother as we brave our way around the corner.

Neighbors are bunched in front of the grocery all packed up like snowballs.

"Here comes Lucy!" Chief Conley waves.

Mr. Lee is pouring out coffee. Mrs. Duffy has her five kids bundled up onto a sled.

Mrs. Kalfo is laughing. “Your grandpa can’t see us. His windows are all iced up.”

There’s the carpenter’s truck, the kids from school—even Miss McCartney’s here.

I take a deep breath and push the door open.

"Where is everybody?" I ask Grandpa, trying to keep the secret.
"Probably at the supermarket," he says. "Who needs this place now?"
"You'd be surprised," I tell my grandpa.

That's when the old front door claps open, cheering for everyone as they come in. Neighbors are carrying paint cans, black and white tiles, nails and hammers, and plaster mix. Some of the people I don't even know.

"What's all this?" my grandpa asks.

"It's Lucy's idea," Mrs. Kalfo says. "We're all here to spruce up this place."

"Did you really think we'd let you get away so fast?" Chief Conley asks my grandpa.

"Who's going to make my deliveries special?" Mr. Lee wants to know.

"And what about our cheese and pickle sandwiches?" the firefighters remind Grandpa.

"And you know me," Mr. Tutti says. "I need yesterday's news today."

"Do you still want this?" I ask Grandpa, taking down the FOR SALE sign.

Grandpa looks around his store. People keep coming in left and right, banging their feet, rubbing their hands, and getting to work. Grandpa walks into the kitchen and comes out holding my colored-in grocery store.

"Thank you, Lucy," he whispers, handing it back to me. "I think your map will need this now." Then Grandpa hugs me, broom and all.

Well, the grand opening of the new supermarket was a huge success. Steven was right. The supermarket is big. But it isn't bigger than a whole neighborhood.

In school Steven pastes a big rectangle on our map and marks it "supermarket."

I raise my hand. "Bigger but not better," I tell Miss McCartney. Then I paste my grandpa's grocery store right around the corner from my house. Milk, juice, butter, eggs—it has everything you need close by. And best of all, it has Grandpa.

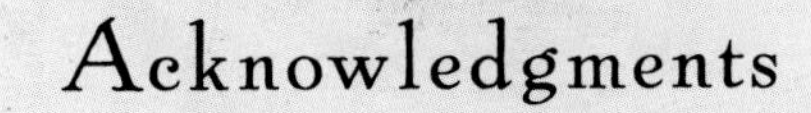

The author would like to acknowledge John Johnson from John's Friendly Market for all his kindness and cooperation.

Endpapers painted by Adrienne Rose Butler and Marja-Lewis Ryan.

Grandpa's Corner Store

Printed in Singapore at Tien Wah Press.

http://www.harperchildrens.com

Library of Congress Cataloging-in-Publication Data
DiSalvo-Ryan, DyAnne.
Grandpa's corner store / DyAnne DiSalvo-Ryan.
p. cm.
Summary: Grandfather's corner grocery business is threatened by a new supermarket, but his granddaughter, Lucy, organizes the neighbors to convince him to stay.
ISBN 0-688-16716-0 (trade)—ISBN 0-688-16717-9 (library)
[1. Grocery trade Fiction. 2. Grandfathers Fiction. 3. Neighborhood Fiction.]
I. Title. PZ7.D6224Gr 2000 [E]—dc21 99-15504 CIP

1 2 3 4 5 6 7 8 9 10

❖

First Edition

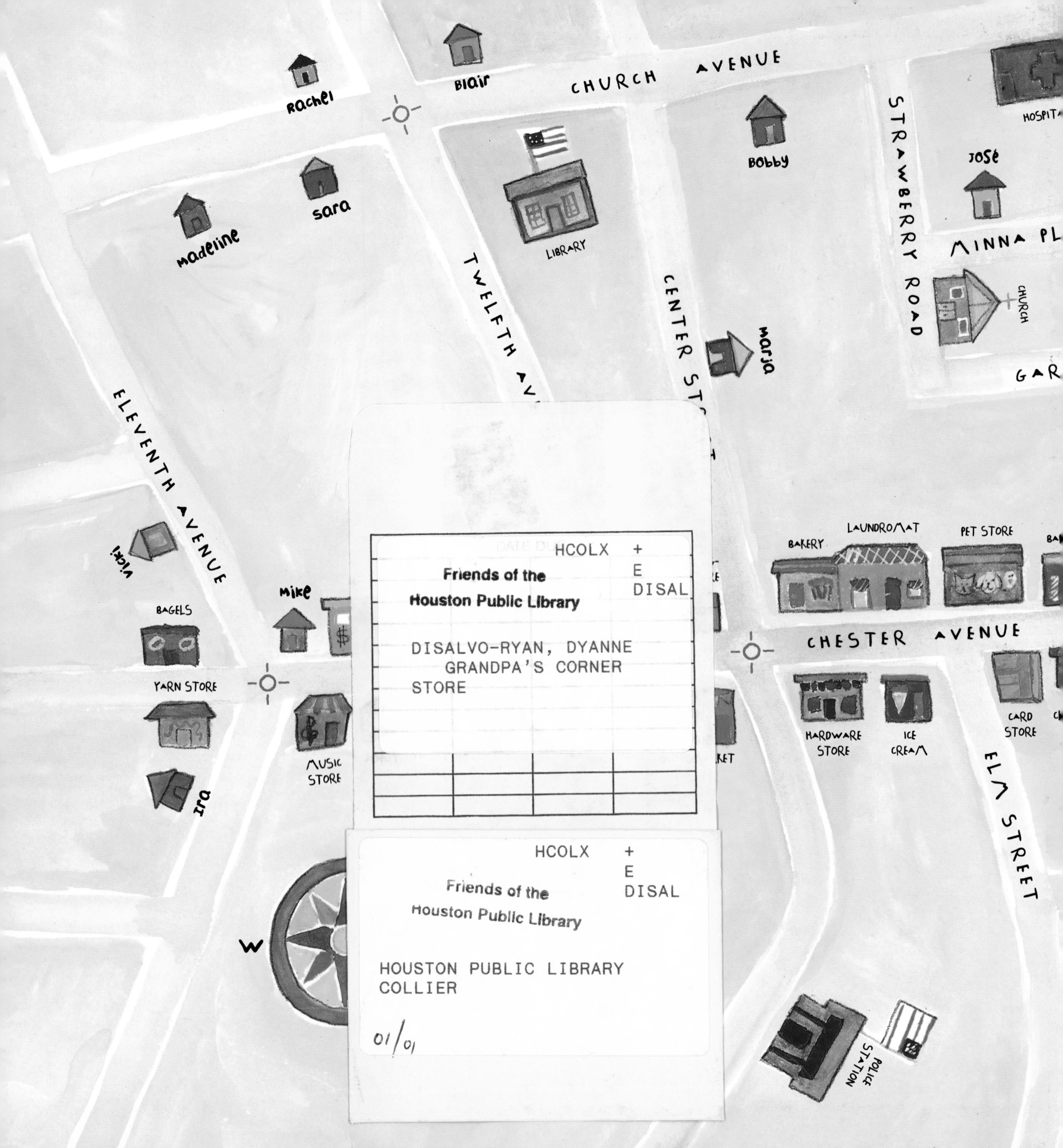
CHURCH AVENUE
Rachel
Blair
Bobby
HOSPIT
José
sara
madeline
LIBRARY
TWELFTH AV
CENTER ST
STRAWBERRY ROAD
MINNA PL
CHURCH
Marja
GAR
ELEVENTH AVENUE
vicki
Mike
BAGELS
YARN STORE
MUSIC STORE
Ira
BAKERY
LAUNDROMAT
PET STORE
CHESTER AVENUE
HARDWARE STORE
ICE CREAM
CARD STORE
ELM STREET
W
POLICE STATION